Dear Parent:
Your child's love of reading starts here!

Every child learns to read in a different way and at his or her own speed. Some go back and forth between reading levels and read favorite books again and again. Others read through each level in order. You can help your young reader improve and become more confident by encouraging his or her own interests and abilities. From books your child reads with you to the first books he or she reads alone, there are I Can Read Books for every stage of reading:

SHARED READING
Basic language, word repetition, and whimsical illustrations, ideal for sharing with your emergent reader

BEGINNING READING
Short sentences, familiar words, and simple concepts for children eager to read on their own

READING WITH HELP
Engaging stories, longer sentences, and language play for developing readers

READING ALONE
Complex plots, challenging vocabulary, and high-interest topics for the independent reader

ADVANCED READING
Short paragraphs, chapters, and exciting themes for the perfect bridge to chapter books

I Can Read Books have introduced children to the joy of reading since 1957. Featuring award-winning authors and illustrators and a fabulous cast of beloved characters, I Can Read Books set the standard for beginning readers.

A lifetime of discovery begins with the magical words **"I Can Read!"**

Visit www.icanread.com for information
on enriching your child's reading experience.

ISBN 978-1-4351-3710-3

Sandy Creek
387 Park Avenue South
New York, NY 10016

Manufactured in China
Manufactured June 2011

Lot 11 12 13 14 15 SCP 10 9 8 7 6 5 4 3 2 1

FOX 2000 PICTURES and REGENCY ENTERPRISES PRESENT A BAGDASARIAN COMPANY PRODUCTION A BETTY THOMAS film "ALVIN AND THE CHIPMUNKS: THE SQUEAKQUEL"
ZACH LEVI DAVID CROSS and JASON LEE and JUSTIN LONG MATTHEW GRAY GUBLER JESSE McCARTNEY AMY POEHLER ANNA FARIS CHRISTINA APPLEGATE
COSTUME DESIGNER ALEXANDRA WELKER EXECUTIVE MUSIC PRODUCER ALI DEE THEODORE MUSIC SUPERVISOR JULIANNE JORDAN MUSIC BY DAVID NEWMAN ANIMATION SUPERVISOR CHRIS BAILEY FILM EDITOR MATTHEW FRIEDMAN
PRODUCTION DESIGNER MARCIA HINDS DIRECTOR OF PHOTOGRAPHY ANTHONY B. RICHMOND, ASC/BSC EXECUTIVE PRODUCERS KAREN ROSENFELT ARNON MILCHAN MICHELE IMPERATO STABILE STEVE WATERMAN
PRODUCED BY JANICE KARMAN ROSS BAGDASARIAN BASED UPON THE CHARACTERS "ALVIN AND THE CHIPMUNKS" CREATED BY ROSS BAGDASARIAN SCREENPLAY BY WILL McROBB AND CHRIS VISCARDI DIRECTED BY BETTY THOMAS

REGENCY   SOUNDTRACK ON RHINO   DOLBY   www.munkyourself.com

Sandy Creek
NEW YORK

Alvin, Simon, and Theodore

were no ordinary chipmunks.

They knew how to sing.

They knew how to dance.

And they knew how to rock and roll.

So when their school
had a singing contest,
Alvin was sure they'd win.

"Who's going to beat singing chipmunks?" said Alvin.

Alvin was so sure The Chipmunks would win the contest that he played football with his cool new friends instead of practicing with his brothers.

Simon wasn't sure they'd win. "I'm kind of a big picture guy," said Simon.

"And the big picture tells me
you can't win if you don't practice,"
he said.

Theodore was sure

they would lose the contest.

"It's one for all

and three for one," said Theodore.

"Without Alvin,

we just aren't The Chipmunks!"

Alvin was the leader
of the band.

He was also the leader
of all the trouble they got into.

Now The Chipmunks
were in deep trouble.

Dave couldn't help.

He was far away in a hospital bed.

He couldn't move!

"What's going on, guys?"

Dave wondered.

He missed The Chipmunks,

but they told him they were okay.

Ian, their old manager, had worked with Alvin, Simon, and Theodore when they first started singing. But Ian only cared about money, so The Chipmunks left him.

"I lost everything," said Ian. "I just hope and pray that somewhere out there are other animals who can sing and dance."

One day,

three of The Chipmunks' biggest fans

came to Los Angeles.

"We made it, girls," said Brittany.

"I can't believe we're really here!"

Brittany, Eleanor, and Jeanette

were no ordinary fans.

They were singers.

They were dancers.

They were The Chipettes!

Brittany was the group's leader.

She led her sisters right

to the basement of Jett Records

where Ian now lived.

"He made The Chipmunks famous,"

she said.

"He can make us stars, too!"

Jeanette wasn't sure of anything.

"I'm Jeanette," she said.

"Although I feel more like an Olivia, or an Emily . . ."

Eleanor wasn't thinking

about singing at all.

She only wanted to know one thing—

"When do you think

we can meet The Chipmunks?"

It was time for the contest.

Would Alvin get back

from the football game in time

to go onstage with The Chipmunks?

Or would The Chipettes

sing and win it all?

All the fans were gathered at the school.

Even Dave made it.

It was time to rock and roll!

The Chipettes began to sing.

Then The Chipmunks joined in.

And when the two groups

performed together,

they were unbeatable!